Text copyright © 2021 by Anne Laurel Carter
Illustrations copyright © 2021 by Akin Duzakin
Published in Canada and the USA in 2021 by Groundwood Books

Groundwood Books / House of Anansi Press
groundwoodbooks.com

Groundwood Books respectfully acknowledges that the land on which we operate is the Traditional Territory of many Nations, including the Anishinabeg, the Wendat and the Haudenosaunee. It is also the Treaty Lands of the Mississaugas of the Credit.

We gratefully acknowledge for their financial support of our publishing program the Canada Council for the Arts, the Ontario Arts Council and the Government of Canada.

Canada Council   Conseil des Arts
for the Arts   du Canada

ONTARIO ARTS COUNCIL
CONSEIL DES ARTS DE L'ONTARIO
an Ontario government agency
un organisme du gouvernement de l'Ontario

With the participation of the Government of Canada | Canadä
Avec la participation du gouvernement du Canada

Library and Archives Canada Cataloguing in Publication
Title: What the kite saw / Anne Laurel Carter ; pictures by Akin Duzakin.
Names: Carter, Anne Laurel, author. | Düzakin, Akin, illustrator.
Identifiers: Canadiana (ebook) 20200285823 | Canadiana (print) 20200285807 | ISBN 9781773062440 (EPUB) | ISBN 9781773065144 (Kindle) | ISBN 9781773062433 (hardcover)
Classification: LCC PS8555.A7727 W53 2021 | DDC jC813/.54—dc23

The illustrations were done in soft pastel, with details in crayon and watercolor.
Design by Michael Solomon
Printed and bound in China

FSC
www.fsc.org
MIX
Paper from responsible sources
FSC® C012700

For Alia, who is a kite.
— ALC

What the Kite Saw

Words by Anne Laurel Carter
Pictures by Akin Duzakin

ⓖ

Groundwood Books / House of Anansi Press
Toronto / Berkeley

WHEN soldiers occupied my town,

they took my father and brother away.

A tank rumbled down the street,
and a loudspeaker voice announced:
"Do not leave your homes.
Cover your windows.
Anyone out on the street will be shot."

The first night of the curfew, Mama made supper.
I couldn't stop staring at the empty places of my father and brother.
My little sister couldn't stop crying, so I drew pictures and told stories
until she fell asleep in Mama's arms.

Then I peered through a crack in the curtains.
Another tank crawled down my street, grinding the stones.
Its spotlight searched the park where I played with my friends.

That night, though I was too old,
I slept on Mama's other side.

In the morning, the loudspeaker voice announced:
"The curfew is lifted for one hour."

I met my friends at the park, swapping stories and kicking a ball,
while Mama shopped.

Night after night, we watched the door,
hoping to see my father and brother.
I drew pictures and told stories,
then peeked out at my town occupied by soldiers.
Sometimes I heard the sharp crack of gunfire.

One night, spotlights climbed the building on the corner.
I heard shouts and gunshots. Someone ran into the street.
I imagined wings so they could fly away.

The next day when the curfew
was lifted,
the wind made the treetops dance
and gave me an idea
that I shared with my friends.

At home, I cut out a big star.
Mama asked what I was making.
"A kite," I said.

After supper, I paced the room and told a story
about everything the kite might see as it flew above our town.

I went up to the rooftop and waited until the tank rumbled by
before I tossed the kite into the air.
It spun and dove into a corner.

The next time I held the kite high, and as I tossed,
I imagined it leaping up to catch a ride on the back of the wind.
The kite rose above our street.

Other kites began to fly over the rooftops.
I heard Mama and my sister clapping, then gunfire.
One by one, the kites fell.

So I cut the string.
The kite darted and danced.
A spotlight briefly chased the rising star
before it disappeared.

Back home in the dark,
I told a story about everything the kite saw —
as it flew high over the land,
toward the sea.

AUTHOR'S NOTE
This story was inspired by Palestinian children. It could
take place anywhere children love to fly kites and are
threatened by war.